HEIDI HECKELBECK
Gets Glasses

By Wanda Coven
Illustrated by Priscilla Burris

LITTLE SIMON
New York London Toronto Sydney New Delhi

LITTLE SIMON
An imprint of Simon & Schuster Children's Publishing Division
1230 Avenue of the Americas, New York, New York 10020
Copyright © 2012 by Simon & Schuster, Inc.
All rights reserved, including the right of reproduction in whole or in part in any form.
LITTLE SIMON is a registered trademark of Simon & Schuster, Inc., and associated colophon is a trademark of Simon & Schuster, Inc.
For information about special discounts for bulk purchases, please contact Simon & Schuster Special Sales at 1-866-506-1949 or business@simonandschuster.com.
The Simon & Schuster Speakers Bureau can bring authors to your live event. For more information or to book an event contact the Simon & Schuster Speakers Bureau at 1-866-248-3049 or visit our website at www.simonspeakers.com.
Manufactured in the United States of America 0516 FFG
10 9 8 7 6 5 4 3
Library of Congress Cataloging-in-Publication Data
Coven, Wanda.
Heidi Heckelbeck gets glasses / by Wanda Coven ; illustrated by Priscilla Burris.
p. cm.
Summary: When she gets glasses, Heidi's friend Lucy gets a lot of attention at school, and eight-year-old Heidi decides that she must have glasses too, until her Aunt Trudy helps her to see that she really does not need them.
ISBN 978-1-4424-4171-2 (pbk. : alk. paper) — ISBN 978-1-4424-4172-9 (hardcover : alk. paper) — ISBN 978-1-4424-4173-6 (ebook)
[1. Eyeglasses—Fiction. 2. Self-acceptance—Fiction. 3. Aunts—Fiction. 4. Family life—Fiction. 5. Schools—Fiction. 6. Witches—Fiction.] I. Burris, Priscilla, ill. II. Title.
PZ7.C83392Hd 2012
[Fic]—dc23
2011023408

CONTENTS

Chapter 1: A BRAND-NEW LOOK 1

Chapter 2: FUZZY WUZZY 13

Chapter 3: CUCKOO! 27

Chapter 4: EYE CANDY! 39

Chapter 5: SCOOPS 51

Chapter 6: WHAT A KLUTZ! 63

Chapter 7: BIRD BREW 77

Chapter 8: BIRDBRAIN 89

Chapter 9: DUMB AND DUMBER 99

Chapter 10: BONKERS! 111

A BRAND-NEW LOOK

Heidi sat at her desk and fiddled with her kitty cat-shaped eraser. *Where's Lucy?* Heidi wondered. Lucy had told her that she had a surprise, and Heidi wanted to be the first to know. She pulled out a strawberry-scented pencil and sharpened it. Heidi looked away for only a moment, and that's exactly when Lucy walked in.

"Ooh!" Heidi heard somebody say.

"Aah!" said somebody else.

A bunch of kids had already gathered around Lucy. *It must be something important,* thought Heidi. She rushed to the door and wiggled her way into the middle of the crowd.

"Surprise!" said Lucy when she saw Heidi.

"Wow!" Heidi said.

"Wow, *what*?" asked Charlie Chen, who had just walked into the classroom.

"Lucy got glasses!" shouted Heidi.

Lucy's glasses had brown frames with pink sparkly flowers at the temples.

"Wait—let me see!" said Melanie Maplethorpe, pushing her way to the front. Melanie must have liked Lucy's glasses, because she didn't say "Ew" or anything else like that.

"They make you look smart," said Stanley Stonewrecker.

"They make you look hip!" said Natalie Newman.

"They make us look like twins!" said Bruce Bickerson, who also wore glasses.

Lucy and Bruce slapped each other five.

Lucky Lucy, thought Heidi. *She's getting so much attention for her new glasses.* Heidi had to admit, Lucy's glasses were really, really cool.

Mrs. Welli clapped her hands as she walked into the classroom. "Please take your seats, boys and girls!"

Everyone scrambled to their desks.

Mrs. Welli noticed Lucy's glasses right away.

"So stylish, Lucy," Mrs. Welli said. "And now you'll be able to see the chalkboard."

"Thanks," Lucy said with a smile.

All day everyone made a big deal about Lucy's glasses.

During English, Mrs. Welli read from a book of poems. Then she asked everyone to write their own. At the end of class Mrs. Welli asked Lucy to read hers out loud. Heidi knew why Lucy got picked. It was because of her new glasses.

Lucy stood in front of the class and pushed her glasses to the top of her nose.

"'Glasses,'" said Lucy. "By Lucy Lancaster."

"With my brand-new glasses,
I can see so far away.
I see my friends and
teachers
   on the playground clear as
day.
   The board's no longer blurry—
   even if I'm in the last row!

And what's best about my glasses is—
I've got a brand-new look to show!"

Everyone clapped and whistled.
Lucy curtsied and returned to her seat.

In art, Lucy got the same kind of attention. Mr. Doodlebee even drew a picture of Lucy with her glasses and hung it on the bulletin board.

I wish Mr. Doodlebee would draw a picture of me, thought Heidi. *The problem is, I don't stand out. I need a new look. . . .*

Heidi smiled to herself. *Aha! I know just how to get one.*

Chapter 2

FUZZY WUZZY

Heidi stood on top of a chair in the kitchen.

"News alert! News alert!" she said.

"What's the story?" Henry asked.

"I want to get glasses!" said Heidi.

"And I want you to get off that chair before you get hurt," said Mom.

Heidi stepped down from the chair.

"But I *really* want glasses," Heidi said.

"How about you have a snack first?" suggested Mom. She placed a plate of maple granola bars and two glasses of milk on the table.

Heidi and Henry dipped their granola bars in the milk.

"So, why on earth do you want glasses?" Mom asked.

"'Cause they're COOL!" said Heidi.

"Glasses help people see," said Mom. "They're not used to make people look cool."

"Movie stars wear sunglasses, and

THEY look cool," Henry said.

"Movie stars wear sunglasses so people won't know who they really are," said Mom.

"AND to make them look COOL!" said Heidi.

Mom sighed.

"Okay, glasses can also make you look cool," said Mom.

"So can I get some?" Heidi asked.

"No," said Mom. "If you want to look cool, wear your beach glasses."

"But my beach glasses are shaped like hearts," said Heidi. "They'll make me look like a five-year-old."

"Hey!" Henry said. "I'm five and I

wouldn't wear those beach glasses if you paid me!"

"See?" said Heidi. "Even Henry knows what's cool."

"Heidi, you're *not* getting glasses," Mom said.

"I have an idea," said Henry. "You can have MY glasses!"

Heidi rolled her eyes—as if her kid brother would have anything she'd actually want.

Henry ran upstairs and came back with a pair of glasses and a hand mirror.

"Try these," said Henry. "I got them at that 3-D dinosaur movie."

"Where are the lenses?" asked Heidi.

"I took them out," Henry said. "You can't see anything with them in— unless you're at the movies."

Heidi put on the glasses.

"Wow," said Henry. "They make you look super-smart!"

"They look kind of clunky," Heidi said, looking in the mirror.

"Well, you're not going to get glasses unless you really need them," said Mom.

"But I DO need them!" Heidi said. "I have six GREAT reasons why I need glasses."

Heidi held up a finger for each reason. "Number one: Glasses will make me look smarter! Number two: Glasses will help me get more friends! Number three: Glasses will help me read poetry better!"

Mom began to empty the dish-washer. She didn't seem interested in Heidi's Six Great Reasons.

"Number four: I'll get my picture on the art room bulletin board! Number five: Glasses will make me look cool! And number six: Glasses will help me see better, because the thing is, I'm having a little trouble seeing."

Mom frowned. "Maybe what you need is an eye test," she said.

"I'll do it," said Henry. He held up two fingers. "How many fingers do I have?"

Heidi squinted. "Nine . . . uh, wait— ten."

"RIGHT!" said Henry, holding up

both his hands. "I DO have ten fingers! But the answer is TWO. I'm afraid you failed the eye test."

That gave Heidi an idea. *Maybe if I pretend to have bad eyesight, then I can score a pair of super-cool glasses!*

Chapter 3

CUCKOO!

Click!

Mrs. Welli snapped a picture of Lucy in her new glasses.

Mrs. Welli always took pictures when something *big* happened. She hung them on a special bulletin board called "The Wall of Fame." All the photos were of kids with missing teeth, except the one of Stanley with a cast on his arm. Heidi had never made the Wall of Fame. But she planned to—very soon.

class room

"All eyes on the chalkboard!" said Mrs. Welli. "This morning we're going to make compound words. We'll put two words together to form one new word. She wrote the first example on the board.

"The words 'class' and 'room' become 'classroom,'" said Mrs. Welli.

Heidi raised her hand.

"Yes, Heidi," Mrs. Welli said.

"Would you please write the words a little bigger?" asked Heidi. "I can't see them from here."

Mrs. Welli wrote the word "cat" in bigger letters on the board. "Can you read this?" she asked.

Heidi squinted and tried to read the word.

"'Car'?" she said, pretending she couldn't see very well.

Everyone giggled.

Then Mrs. Welli wrote the word "nip" in slightly bigger letters on the board. "Try this one."

"'Nap'?" Heidi asked.

The class laughed harder.

"Come see me after school," said Mrs. Welli.

At the end of the day Heidi went to see her teacher. Mrs. Welli had written a note for Heidi's parents.

"Heidi, this is very important," Mrs. Welli said. "I want you to give this letter to your mother and father when you get home."

Heidi nodded. Then she skipped all the way to the bus. *YES!* Heidi said to herself. *I fooled my teacher! Now all I have to do is fool Mom and Dad—and*

maybe an eye doctor. Then I can get a
cool pair of glasses!

When she got home from school,
Heidi gave the note to her mom. By
dinner her parents had made Heidi
an eye appointment for the next day
after school.

"Uh-oh," said Henry. "Doctors give much harder eye tests than I do."

"Dr. Chen is nice," Mom said. "Heidi, isn't his son, Charlie, in your class?"

Heidi hadn't heard a word of the conversation. She was daydreaming about how she would look in her new glasses.

"Heidi?" said Mom.

"Anybody home?" Dad asked.

"Have you gone deaf, too?" asked Henry.

"Sure," Heidi said dreamily. "I'd love some more potatoes."

Henry shook his head. "She's not blind OR deaf," he said. "She's just plain CUCKOO!"

Chapter 4

EYE CANDY!

"Have a seat," said Dr. Chen.

Dr. Chen had large ears and spiky black hair. Heidi recognized him from school. Today he looked more like a doctor than a dad. He had on glasses with black frames and wore a white lab coat.

39

Heidi and her mom sat down.

"Heidi, how long have your eyes been bothering you?" Dr. Chen asked.

Heidi tried not to make her story sound too fishy. "I've been seeing fuzzy for a while," she said. "But it really began to bother me a few days ago."

Dr. Chen nodded. "Well, let's take a look," he said.

First, Heidi had to read an eye chart. Dr. Chen gave her something that looked like a black plastic lollipop and asked her to cover one eye with it.

"Now please read line four," said Dr. Chen.

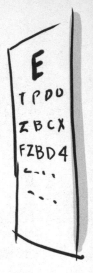

Heidi saw four letters and a number—F Z B D 4—but she didn't read them that way.

"Uh . . . *E, S, R, O,* seven," Heidi said. Dr. Chen looked puzzled. He asked Heidi to read two more lines. She covered the other eye and did the same thing. *I better not read them ALL wrong,* thought Heidi, *or Dr. Chen will think I've gone completely blind.*

Then Dr. Chen shined a light in Heidi's eyes. He told her to look up and down and from side to side.

Next he asked her to peek into what looked like a viewfinder.

Heidi liked viewfinders. She had tried one on a family camping trip.

Her family had hiked up a mountain,
and Heidi had spotted a viewfinder at
the top. Dad had given her quarters
to put inside. She had spied villages,
lakes, and churches from up high.

But inside Dr. Chen's viewfinder,
Heidi only saw a bunch of letters.
Dr. Chen fiddled with the viewfinder
and asked Heidi if the letters looked
better or worse. Heidi would answer

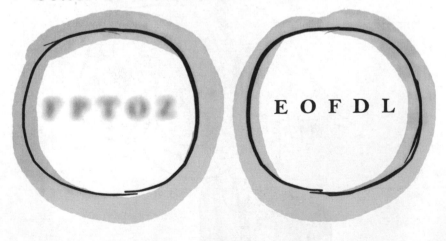

"worse" when the letters looked better and "better" when the letters looked worse. Soon the tests were over.

"Well, Heidi," said Dr. Chen, "it looks like you're going to need glasses."

"That's great news!" Heidi said.

"I'm glad you feel that way," said Dr. Chen.

Dr. Chen took Heidi to the next room. There were racks and racks

of brightly colored glasses. *It's like a candy store!* thought Heidi. *Only better!* She chose a pair of black glasses with glitter inside the plastic— like sparkly gems inside a rock. She tried them on.

"Super-funky," said Heidi, looking in the mirror. Then she turned to her

mom. "What do you think?"

"They're very *you*," said Mom, who still couldn't get used to the idea that Heidi needed glasses.

The lady behind the counter told Heidi she was going to get her new glasses ready. While she waited, Heidi did a connect-the-dots puzzle, four hidden pictures, and two word searches. It felt like she had been waiting forever, when suddenly . . .

"Heidi Heckelbeck?" called the lady from behind the counter.

Heidi jumped up from her seat.

Finally! she thought. *I can't wait to wear my new glasses. They're going to make me look SO cool.* But when Heidi put them on, she discovered that there was a teeny-weeny problem.

She couldn't see a thing.

Chapter 5

SCOOPS

Heidi took off her glasses on the way to the car. *These glasses are hurting my eyes,* she thought. *Maybe I shouldn't have lied so much about the lines on the eye chart.*

"Put your glasses back on," said Mom. "You need to wear them in order to get used to them."

Heidi listened to her mom and put them back on. She slid them a little way down her nose. *That's better. Now I can see over the top.*

"No cheating," said Mom.

"Okay," said Heidi as she slid the glasses back in place.

Mom pulled into a shopping plaza

and parked in front of Scoops—Heidi's favorite ice-cream shop.

"Surprise!" said Mom. "I thought we would celebrate your new glasses with ice cream."

Heidi saw Dad and Henry waving from inside the shop.

"Thanks, Mom!" said Heidi.

She hopped out of the car and lifted her glasses so she wouldn't trip on the curb. Then she put them back in place when she got inside.

Dad patted Heidi on the back.

"You look so grown-up," Dad said.

"You look more like you're playing dress-up," said Henry.

"Very funny," Heidi said. "But these are the REAL thing."

Heidi handed her glasses to Henry, and he put them on.

"Whoa!" said Henry. "I can't see a thing!"

"I told you I needed glasses," said Heidi as she put them back on.

Then they went to order ice cream.

"What can I get for you?" asked a girl in a Scoops T-shirt.

Heidi looked at the menu on the back wall. She couldn't read any of the flavors, and she couldn't sneak a

peek from under her glasses because her whole family was watching.

"I'll try a scoop of that one," Heidi said, pointing to the special of the day.

"I'll have Moose Tracks," said Henry.

After they got their cones, Dad grabbed napkins and they headed outside.

Heidi took a lick of her cone. "Ew!" she said. "It tastes like pineapple."

"Duh," Henry said. "Because that's what you ordered."

Merg, thought Heidi. But she didn't make a big deal about ordering the wrong ice cream. She didn't want her family to wonder what was wrong with her glasses. Heidi looked for a wastebasket to pitch her cone into, and then . . . *bonk!* She bumped into Henry and—*squash!*—his cone smushed right into his nose.

Henry began to whine.

"I'm sorry, little buddy. I didn't

mean to," said Heidi. "Here, you can have mine."

Heidi offered her cone to Henry, but he pushed it away. She shrugged and tossed her cone in the trash.

"What a fiasco!" said Mom as she wiped ice cream off Henry's face.

"What's that mean?" asked Henry.

"It means that this ice-cream trip almost turned into a disaster," said Dad.

Heidi began to wonder if her new glasses might be a fiasco too, but she pushed that thought right out of her head.

Chapter 6

WHAT A KLUTZ!

The next morning Heidi made a grand entrance at school.

"One! Two! Three!" she counted.

Then she burst into the classroom.

Nobody looked.

"AHEM," said Heidi as she made her way toward her desk.

Still nobody looked—until . . .

Whump! Heidi bumped smack into Melanie. Melanie's armful of books tumbled to the floor.

"Hey! Watch where you're going, weirdo!" Melanie said.

"Uh, sorry," said Heidi. "I'm still getting used to my new glasses."

Heidi helped Melanie pick up her books.

"Since when do YOU wear glasses?" Melanie asked.

"Since yesterday," said Heidi. "So, what do you think?"

Melanie took a close look at Heidi.

"Black is not a good color for you," said Melanie. "But I like the sparkles."

Coming from Melanie, that was a compliment.

"Thanks," said Heidi, before she continued on to her desk.

Then—*bonk!*—Heidi crashed into her chair and knocked it over. It clanked on the floor. This time everyone looked. *Finally!* thought Heidi as she picked up her chair. Lucy and Bruce ran to Heidi's desk.

"You got glasses!" Lucy said.

"Why didn't you tell us?" asked Bruce.

"I didn't find out until yesterday that I was getting them," explained Heidi. "Do you like them?"

"I love them!" said Lucy.

"They're super-cool," Bruce said.

"Thanks," said Heidi. "Now we can be triplets!"

Heidi, Lucy, and Bruce high-fived.
Heidi mostly slapped air because
everything was so fuzzy.

Everyone swarmed around Heidi
until Mrs. Welli asked the class to take
their seats.

"Heidi, your glasses look lovely,"
said Mrs. Welli. "Come see me during
snack time, and I'll take your picture."

Heidi nodded.

That means I'm going to make the Wall of Fame! thought Heidi. She felt so important. The only problem was, she couldn't see much with her new glasses.

When Heidi wrote in her journal, her sentences came out slanted. In art, the class had to draw a bowl of fruit. Heidi's looked more like a bowl of garbage.

My glasses help me see better.

"Why did you paint red bananas and purple apples?" asked Lucy.

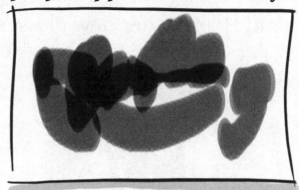

"Those are bananas?" Bruce asked.

"Mr. Doodlebee called it 'artistic interpretation,'" said Heidi.

"What's that?" Lucy asked.

"It means that the artist has completely lost her marbles," replied Melanie.

Heidi covered her ears to drown out

the laughter. To make matters worse, Mr. Doodlebee didn't even draw a picture of Heidi in her new glasses.

At lunch Heidi bumped into the table with her tray. She took off her glasses so she could wipe up the juice that had spilled all over.

"Are you *sure* you need glasses?" questioned Lucy.

Heidi shoved her glasses back on. "Of course I'm sure," she said. "I'm just getting used to them."

"Mine felt good on the very first day," said Lucy.

"Well, lucky for you!" said Heidi.

Lucy and Bruce gave each other a look. Heidi pretended not to notice.

At dinner that night Heidi poured milk all over the floor.

"You're such a klutz!" said Henry.

"Am not!"

"Are too!"

"Enough," said Dad.

"Heidi," said Mom, "are your new glasses bothering you?"

"No," lied Heidi. "I love them."

But the truth was, Heidi's eyeballs were killing her. She skipped dessert and went to her room. That night Heidi fell sound asleep in her tights, shoes, clothes—everything except her glasses, which had fallen on the floor.

Chapter 7

BiRD BREW

Heidi peeked out from under her covers. Had she dreamed she had gotten glasses? No such luck. There they were on her bedside table. Someone had picked them up during the night.

Then Heidi's door burst open.

"Race you downstairs!" shouted Henry. "Dad made apple fritters for Saturday breakfast."

Heidi pulled the sheet over her head. Henry was too loud, too happy, and way too awake for her. *But since it's Saturday,* she thought, *I get to visit Aunt Trudy.* Heidi loved her aunt Trudy. She taught Heidi spells and showed her how to use her gifts as a witch.

Heidi got out of bed and got ready for the day. After brushing her teeth, she put on her black jeans and her I ♥ BABY ANIMALS T-shirt. Then she trotted downstairs with her glasses in her pocket.

"I'm off to Aunt Trudy's," Heidi said as she grabbed an apple fritter.

"Be back for lunch," said Mom. "Remember, Lucy's coming over. And don't forget to wear your glasses."

Heidi nodded. On her way to Aunt Trudy's she nibbled her apple fritter and kicked an acorn along the sidewalk. *It sure is nice to be able to see,* Heidi thought. When she got to Aunt Trudy's, she put on her glasses and rang the bell.

"Oh my," said Aunt Trudy as

she opened the door. "Don't *you* look smart!"

Aunt Trudy gave Heidi a big hug. Her aunt smelled like flowers—because she had her own perfume business. Heidi followed Aunt Trudy into the kitchen. She peeked out from under her glasses so she wouldn't trip.

"You know what's odd?" asked Aunt Trudy.

"What?" Heidi said.

"None of the witches in our family have ever needed glasses. I mean, sometimes I use magnifying glasses to read very fine print, but that's not the same as real glasses."

Heidi shrugged, then changed the subject. "What are these?" she asked, picking up one of the little bottles on the kitchen table.

"Those bottles are for Percy," said
Aunt Trudy.

Percy was Aunt Trudy's beloved
parrot. Most of his feathers were
bright red, and his wings were yellow
and blue.

"Is Percy okay?" Heidi asked.

"I'm afraid he's under the weather," said Aunt Trudy. "Would you like to mix him a get-well potion?"

"Would I ever!" said Heidi.

"Then let's get right to work," said Aunt Trudy.

She opened her *Book of Spells* and placed it in front of Heidi.

Heidi did her best to figure out the words with her glasses on. "Bird stew?" she asked uncertainly.

Aunt Trudy laughed. "No, silly.

We're going to make Percy a get-well *brew*."

"Oh—I see," Heidi said.

"Well, I should hope so, with those fancy new glasses!" said Aunt Trudy.

87

Chapter 8

BiRDBRAiN

Aunt Trudy lifted Percy out of his cage and set him on his perch. Heidi measured the ingredients.

Three tablespoons of pepper, Heidi read to herself—or at least, that's what she thought she read. Heidi measured three tablespoons of pepper and

dumped them in the bowl. She tried
to read the next ingredient. *Eight*

*tablespoons of ground sunflower
seeds—or is that a three?* Heidi
wondered. *No, it looks
more like an eight.* She
added the seeds to
the mix and

looked at the next item. *A half cup of maple syrup.* Heidi poured the maple syrup into the mix and stirred it together.

"The brew's ready," Heidi said.

"Good work," said Aunt Trudy.

Aunt Trudy picked up the bowl and brushed the brew on Percy's feathers. Then she held her Witches of Westwick medallion in her left hand and placed her right hand over Percy.

She chanted the words of the spell.

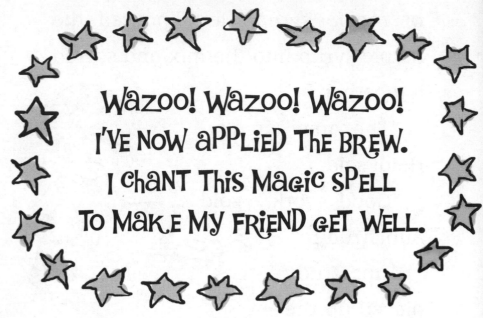

WAZOO! WAZOO! WAZOO!
I'VE NOW APPLIED THE BREW.
I CHANT THIS MAGIC SPELL
TO MAKE MY FRIEND GET WELL.

Percy ruffled his feathers and squawked.

"Are you feeling better, sweet boy?" asked Aunt Trudy.

Percy squawked again.

Then something odd happened.

Percy began to grow.

He grew and grew and GREW.

Crack!

Percy's perch snapped in two, and
he kept on growing.

He became the size
of a cat.

Then the size of a
dog. Soon he was as

large as a pony.

"Oh, goodness
me!" Aunt Trudy
cried nervously.

"What's happening?" asked Heidi.

"It seems that
something's gone
wrong with our

get-well brew," said Aunt Trudy. She
grabbed the *Book of Spells* and began
to read the ingredients out loud.

"Eight tablespoons of pepper . . ."

"No, three," corrected Heidi.

"And three tablespoons of ground
sunflower seeds . . ."

"No, eight," Heidi said.

Aunt Trudy handed the book to Heidi and folded her arms. Heidi took off her glasses and read the ingredients. She had mistaken the number three for the number eight and the number eight for the number three. *Oh no,* thought Heidi. *I totally blew it.*

"Br-r-r-r-ock!" squawked Percy, whose head now touched the ceiling.

Chapter 9

DUMB AND DUMBER

Heidi felt like a complete birdbrain.
Percy was the size of an elephant.
Aunt Trudy was afraid he might grow
even more and burst through the roof.
She had to reverse the spell—and fast.
Aunt Trudy held her medallion in her
left hand and chanted:

Wazoo! Wazoo! Wazee!
Please let this bird be free!
We made a blunder —
most unwise.
Now make this bird
a normal size!

Swoosh! A great gust of wind swirled around Percy.

"B-r-r-r—ock!" he squawked.

Heidi covered her eyes. Some of the potion bottles on the table clinked and fell over. Then it became quiet.

"You can look," Aunt Trudy said.

Heidi peeked between her fingers.
Percy was sitting on the kitchen table.
He was just the right size for a parrot.
Heidi stroked his head with her finger.

"I'm glad he didn't go through the
roof," said Heidi.

"Me too," said Aunt Trudy. "But he still needs the bird brew treatment."

Heidi whipped up another batch of the bird brew and brushed it on Percy. This time she didn't wear her glasses, and this time Heidi chanted the spell herself. *I hope it works,* she thought.

When she had finished chanting, she looked at Percy.

Percy fluffed his feathers and flew onto Heidi's shoulder.

"He's nuzzling my hair," said Heidi.

"That's his way of saying thank you," said Aunt Trudy.

Heidi and Aunt Trudy laughed.

Then Aunt Trudy picked up Heidi's glasses. "So what's the story behind these?" she asked.

Heidi bit her lip. "The story is . . . ," Heidi began. "The story is . . . I never really needed glasses."

"I *knew* it!" said Aunt Trudy. "None of the Witches of Westwick have ever

needed glasses." Then she looked into Heidi's eyes. "So what's the *rest* of the story?"

"I wanted to be cool," Heidi said.

Aunt Trudy laughed.

"What's so funny?" asked Heidi.

"It reminds me of when I was your age," said Aunt Trudy. "I wanted to be cool too, so one time I wore a strip of tinfoil on my top teeth for a whole day."

"Why?"

"Because I thought braces were cool."

"So you made fake braces out of tinfoil?" Heidi asked.

"That's right," said Aunt Trudy.

Heidi laughed. "That's even dumber than what I did!"

"Well, I'd say it's more of a tie," said Aunt Trudy with a wink.

"Yeah, maybe," Heidi said.

"And let's be thankful we don't need glasses *or* braces," said Aunt Trudy. "And above all, remember this. . . ."

"What?"

"That you already are a very special girl. Just think—how many girls have special powers like you?"

"None that I know of," said Heidi.

Aunt Trudy gave Heidi a big hug. Then Heidi shoved her glasses into her pocket and skipped all the way home for lunch.

Chapter 10

BONKERS!

"Heiii-diii!" called Dad from the back door. "Lucy's here!"

Heidi and Henry had just found four rocks to hold down the corners of the tablecloth on the picnic table. They put the rocks in place and ran to the house.

"The picnic food is all ready," said Dad.

Heidi carried a platter of sandwiches. Lucy carried the brownies. Henry got the chips. Dad grabbed two bottles of his homemade fizzy lemonade, and Mom brought plates, napkins, and cups.

They all sat at the picnic table under the shade of a maple tree.

"Everything looks so good!" said Heidi.

"How do you know?" asked Henry. "You're not wearing your glasses."

"Who needs glasses?" Heidi asked.

Everyone stared at Heidi.

"What do you mean?" asked Lucy.

"Well, the truth is," said Heidi. "I don't really *need* glasses."

"You're kidding!" said Dad.

"I wondered!" said Mom.

"I KNEW it!" said Henry.

"So why'd you get them?" asked Lucy.

"Because I wanted to be cool, like you and Bruce," Heidi said.

"Wow—you must be CRAZY!" said Lucy. "Because I wish I *didn't* need glasses."

"No, YOU'RE crazy!" said Heidi. "Because glasses look really good on you."

"You know what?" Henry said. "You're BOTH crazy!"

"That means we must be TWINS!" said Heidi.

Heidi and Lucy slapped each other five.

Henry rolled his eyes. "See what I mean? TOTALLY bonkers."

"Heidi may be a little bonkers," said Dad, "but she's also very special."

"It's true," said Mom, giving Heidi a hug. "You don't need glasses to make you more special. We love you just the way you are."

Heidi opened her desk and found a blank piece of paper with a happy-face border on top of her math book. The paper was crinkly in the middle, like it had been wet. Heidi sniffed it.

An excerpt from *Heidi Heckelbeck and the Secret Admirer*

The paper smelled like lemons. It had a folded note attached to it with a paper clip. Heidi undid the paper clip. A few scratch-'n'-sniff candy stickers floated to the bottom of her desk. *Can this be from my secret admirer?* wondered Heidi. Then she unfolded the note and read it.

Hold the paper with the happy faces close to a lightbulb and find a secret message.

"Hei-di!" called Mrs. Welli. "Kindly close your desk and pay attention."

Heidi shoved the note, the stickers, and the piece of paper inside her math book and closed the lid of her desk. Then she tried to work on double-digit subtraction, but she couldn't stop thinking about the note. *Who can it be from? Maybe it's Charlie Chen. Charlie's working on a lemon battery, and the paper smells like lemons. Plus Charlie gave me a cookie yesterday. It HAS to be Charlie!*

During silent reading Heidi took her secret message—and a book— to the reading corner. She switched on a lamp and held the paper to the light. The message said:

You're as sweet as a sugar beet!

From,
Your Secret Admirer

PS: I'm not a poet, and I know it.

Heidi quickly stuck the paper back inside her book and sat in the Comfy Chair. *I never knew Charlie liked me,* thought Heidi. *I'll have to thank him for all the cool stuff.*

In art Heidi tapped Charlie on the shoulder. He was molding a swan out of clay.

"I really liked your poem," said Heidi.

"What are you talking about?" he asked.

"Didn't you leave a poem and stickers in my desk?" asked Heidi.

"Huh?" he asked.

"Oh, uh, never mind," said Heidi. "Gotta go."

Heidi returned to her seat. *If Charlie isn't my secret admirer, then who can it be?*